Be In The M t

by Janice Hansan

Illustrations by
Mike Motz

Be In The Moment

by **Janice Hansan**   Illustrations by
Mike Motz

My cell is all charged, Son.
I'm staring at the screen.
I'll put it down when I'm done, Son,
And you'll have a full stomach then.

I need to take my selfie, Son.
It is still all about me.
I will protect your identity, Son
And take them only of me.

My cell is all charged, Son.
The pictures are all on my screen.
I just need to send this text, Son.
But wait . . . You're gone!

Is your cell all charged up, Dad?
Are you almost out out of juice?
When will you put it down, Dad?
Well? When?

Your cell is all charged, Dad.
You're staring at the darn screen.
When will you watch the game, Dad?
Huh? When?

My cell's all charged, Dad,
And you're still staring at your screen.
Now it's my turn, Dad.
See you when I sneak back in.

My cell is all charged, Dad.
It is all about me.
I got my graduation selfie, Dad.
Now I know how to be.

I'm all charged up, Dad,
Trying to be in the moment.
Need to take a selfie with my wife, Dad
Then maybe we can get one in.